STRANDED

JUST FOR BOYS® Presents

STRANDED

Ann Coleridge

Illustrated by

ERIC DAVID

Delacorte Press

This book is a presentation of **Just For Boys**®, Weekly Reader
Books. Weekly Reader Books offers book clubs for children
from preschool through high school. For further information
write to: **Weekly Reader Books,** 4343 Equity Drive,
Columbus, Ohio 43228.

Published by arrangement with Delacorte Press. Just For
Boys and Weekly Reader are federally registered trademarks
of Field Publications.

Published by Delacorte Press
Bantam Doubleday Dell Publishing Group, Inc.
666 Fifth Avenue
New York, New York 10103

This work was originally published in Australia
by Angus & Robertson Publishers.

Library of Congress Cataloging in Publication Data
Coleridge, Ann.
Stranded / Ann Coleridge: illustrated by Eric David.
  p.   cm.
Summary: Tony joins in a dangerous mission to roll
several stranded whales back into the sea.
  ISBN: 0-385-29825-0
  [1. Whales—Fiction.]   I. David, Eric, ill.   II. Title.
PZ7.C67727St   1989
[Fic]—dc19   89-1191
                                              CIP
Manufactured in the United States of America   AC

October 1989

10   9   8   7   6   5   4   3   2   1

BG

For O.E.G.

CHAPTER

1

~~~~~~~~~~

A CLEAR, FINE DAWN, but definitely a day for a sweater.
Tony pulled it on, then crept into the kitchen to cut himself
a piece of bread; hardly a slice—more a wedge, with a
substantial crust bordering one side and tapering to a deli-
cate, flimsy fringe on the other. No need for margarine or
jam; the bread was tasty enough as it was. He untangled a
plastic tote bag from the mess stuffed in the cupboard
under the sink and, taking this and his half-eaten wedge,
let himself quietly out the back door. His parents' curtains
were still drawn. They wouldn't stay in bed much longer
themselves, even though it was Sunday, but they wouldn't
thank him for waking them unnecessarily.

The grass was wet with dew. His shoes, soon dark and
sodden, chilled his feet, but the effect was quite pleasur-
able, combining with the deep breaths of tangy air to
awaken all his senses from their night's sleep. The air was
as crisp and cool as a lettuce; there would be sunshine
later. As he left the grass and started down the gentle slope
to the beach, his shoes acquired a leprous coating of sand.

Head bowed, he was already scanning the sand at his
feet for things of interest. He had in the past found keys, a
toy car, several coins, and a wonderful range of combs,
some with missing or bent teeth, but some quite service-
able. This morning, however, he saw only bull ants and
small snails among the marram grass. Down on the beach
he swallowed the last of his bread and turned to walk along
the high-tide line, peering closely at this morning's offering

left by the sea. There were abalone shells, which he had once collected in handfuls because he couldn't resist the muted rainbows shining in their mother-of-pearl; now he had so many at home that he would only collect a new one if it was a particularly fine specimen, and on the understanding, demanded by his mother, that he would throw out one of his lesser specimens for each new one he brought home. He found a cone shell, sleek and speckled. The man at the local shop would pay him thirty cents for this. It would then be sold for twice as much, but Tony had learned from experience that it was a case of, "Take it or leave it, son; I'm doing you a favor, really." He wanted desperately to find a paper nautilus. He knew the shopkeeper would give him five dollars for one, but if he found one, he would keep it. It would stand on the top of his bookcase and he would be able to see it as he lay in bed. Its intense whiteness would be visible except on the darkest of nights. Twice he had found paper nautilus fragments, which had tantalized him with the knowledge that it was possible that he would one day find a complete specimen.

He picked up a stick of driftwood so that he could turn over the clumps of seaweed that might be concealing something interesting. Their surface was beginning to dry out, but the sand underneath was still dark with moisture. Sand fleas sprang up and down on the disturbed weed as if they were having a tantrum. The smell under the weed was strong. He poked about with the stick, not wanting to put his fingers among the strands. There was always the danger of broken glass, but far more unnerving was the possibility of unexpectedly touching a decaying fish or octopus. He already had a small octopus at home. Mom had pickled it in formalin and put it in a screwtop jar, which was not on his chest of drawers. She had wanted to put the jar among the gherkins and pickled onions to give Dad a surprise, but Tony had been so frightened that Dad might eat it, or at least cut into it without thinking, that he had begged her not to.

2

He passed an empty beer can. He would collect it on the way back and add it to the bag of cans he was going to take to the recycling depot. Still bent over, as if in extreme old age, he continued slowly along the beach. By now he had two more cone shells and a cowrie in his bag. The cowrie was for Mom. She loved all shapes, sizes, and colors of cowries without being able to explain why. She didn't put them out on a shelf, because she said she had quite enough dusting to do as it was. Instead, she kept them in a box, where she very seldom saw them, but she said that she loved them just the same.

The circle of his vision was small. Scrutinizing the ragged line of motley offerings from the night's high tide, he saw each small area with intense clarity. Reflected morning light shafted from the glassy faces of individual sand grains. Each shadow or protuberance on the flat terrain had to be investigated in case it signaled the presence of some hidden trophy.

Outside this slowly progressing spotlight of his concentration, all else remained unseen. Thus it was that the stark white of the paper nautilus that lay free on the surface of the sand in his path didn't enter his vision until his feet were within a yard of it. Crisp and chalky, like a starched and goffered Elizabethan ruff, it had survived the pounding and tumbling of the waves and lay intact. Picking it up, he turned it over and over in his hands, gently brushing the sand from its delicately fluted contours. Not a crack nor a blemish. Perfection.

"You beautiful, beautiful thing. At last."

There was no point in going on any further this morning. Tony wanted to take the precious nautilus home right away before it came to any harm. He would rinse it in tap water and put it safely on his bookcase. For the first time since he had come down onto the beach, he straightened his back and looked around him.

About a hundred yards farther along the beach, just at the water's edge, was a low, dark shape. At first sight he thought it was a large bundle, but then he realized that his view of it was foreshortened by being seen partially end-on. It was tapered at each end. An upside-down canoe? Perhaps there had been an accident farther along the coast. He started toward it, half running but half walking since he was aware of the precious paper nautilus he held in his hand, too precious to be put in the tote bag with the other shells.

As he drew nearer to the black object, he thought he saw it move slightly—or was it just his own movement as he jogged over the sand? He stopped and stood very still. This time there was a wild thrashing at one end—a tail. It was alive, then. A monstrous fish lyin ; on its side parallel with the water line. But what fish could be so large? A shark? He approached cautiously now. The thrashing stopped. The creature was massive, at least three yards long. Its head was not pointed at the front but rounded and fleshy.

Best not to get too near. It was presumably dying. He walked around it at a safe distance.

For the first time that morning he was conscious of sounds . . . the quiet lapping of the sea, the cry of gulls, the sporadic crackling among the patches of stranded sea-weed as they dried in the cold breeze, and a regular blowing and occasional plaintive squeaking from the fish itself. Tony noticed a hole in the top of its head. The hole opened explosively and shut again—a blowhole. Not a fish, then, but a whale.

Tony now saw that the tail was set so that it would be horizontal in the water—not vertical like a fish's tail. Yes, definitely a whale. In that case it wasn't dying but just stranded. Next time the tide came in, it could swim out to sea. Meanwhile it would just lie quietly on the beach, breathing air through its blowhole. One problem, though, might be dogs. During the day they would roam the beach— might they attack the defenseless creature? Tony decided to guard it and keep it company during its long wait for the tide. His parents would guess where he was. If they started

to worry when he didn't return, they would come to look for him. They might be angry at first, but when they knew about the whale, they would understand.

The whale flexed its back and emitted more frenzied squeaks. Tony gazed down into the still depths of the one visible eye. He felt that the whale's consciousness, its being, was down inside the eye.

"Hello, whale," he said, then quickly looked around, dreading being caught doing anything quite so foolish as standing on a deserted beach talking to one end of a three-yard whale. Reassured that nobody was in sight, still less within hearing range, he sat down near the whale's head, resting his bag of shells on the sand while still holding the paper nautilus.

"You'll be all right. I'm afraid it'll seem an awfully long time before the tide comes in, but I'll look after you."

After all, he thought defiantly, people talk to their cats and dogs, so what's so crazy about talking to a whale? After a while, though, it became difficult to think of anything to say, like visiting someone in the hospital. He told the whale about each of the shells, then thought perhaps he had done enough talking for a bit. The eye was looking at him, but perhaps it couldn't look anywhere else, stuck there like that. The pitiful squeaking still came and went. He sang it a song. There was quite a strong wind now, penetrating through the wool of his sweater and blowing against the dry skin of the whale. Tony smoothed a patch of sand and drew a whale on it, adding a boat, a mermaid, three seagulls, and an island with palm trees. He drew a Spitfire and a Stuka. The Stuka dive-bombed the mermaid, who went up in a cloud of sand. He drew a family for the whale in the picture—a wife, a baby, and an old grandfather whale. A man had bailed out of the Spitfire and was coming down by parachute. As he drew, Tony became aware of a quiet, rhythmic thumping, which he seemed to hear through the sand. He peered at the eye of the whale lying in front of him. Perhaps the thumping was its heart,

6

beating loudly and quickly now because it was angry or frightened. Tony got up and moved away slightly.

Standing, he saw a figure jogging steadily toward him, a man whose feet were pounding along on the sand with a steady thumping sound. Beside him bounded a terrier. Tony recognized Howard, one of the local boatbuilders.

"Hi, Tony," called Howard. "Is it still alive? *Quiet*, Ruff!" He grabbed the dog and put it on a leash.

"I think so," Tony answered. "At least, it was just now. What sort is it?"

"Sit, Ruff, sit. I dunno. Look, you're supposed to keep them wet. That one's dried right out; look at its skin. What with this wind, and the sun later, he'll start blistering and cracking pretty soon."

"I didn't know, I'm sorry."

"Look, we've got to get it back into the sea before they all come. We're going to need help for that. Get down, will ya, yer stupid dog!"

"Before who all come?"

"The other whales. Look, we must hurry. Run to the houses and bang on a few doors. No, on second thought I'll have to go, so that I can get rid of this darn dog—the whale's made him go crazy. You stay here and keep the whale wet. You can fetch water in that bag. Don't fill it too full or the handles'll bust. You'll just have to keep going back to the sea for small amounts. Wet all over, mind; he could die and crack open in the sun, poor old beggar. Mind the blowhole, though; no water near that, or you'll drown him. See you later."

Howard grabbed the protesting dog and carried it a short distance back along the beach before setting it down, still on the leash. Then he pounded off into the distance, the terrier yapping and scampering at his side.

"What other whales?" said Tony to the eye. "Why are they coming? What about my shells? And the nautilus? I'm sorry, I didn't know you were going to get too dry."

He reached out tentatively and touched the whale's

skin—lightly with one fingertip at first, then more confidently with his whole hand. The skin was soft to the touch, but gritty, too, where blowing sand had clung to it.

"Poor old beggar," repeated Tony. "Never mind, you'll soon be okay."

A little way farther up the beach he tipped the shells out of the bag and placed the paper nautilus carefully on top. Down at the sea's edge again, he dipped the bag into the water. It wasn't easy; the two sides of the bag tended to cling together and float on the top. The movement of the expanse of plastic on the slight eddies of the water made it difficult for him to control the top edge of the bag and keep one side out of the water while forcing the other side down under the surface. Once he had started getting the water in, it was difficult to stop the bag from overfilling. The first time he started to lift it from the water, the plastic bulged and strained dangerously, and he had to use one hand to pull the bottom upward and tip some water out, while holding both handles with the other hand. The swollen bag bent in the middle, and too much water tipped out. Still, what was left was better than nothing, and he ran back to the whale with it, pouring it in a trickle along the whale's flank. It flowed onto the sand below the whale, its path down the whale's skin being marked by a slight dampness.

Tony went back to the water and went through the same laborious process of trying to coax a reasonable amount of water into the bag.

What I need's a bucket, he thought as he returned to the whale and tipped the water onto the front part of its head. *Or a couple of beer cans*, remembering the one he had passed. *No, it would take too long going back to fetch it, and anyway the can's hopelessly small*. He dipped the bag in the water and returned to the whale, pouring the water over another section of its flank. The patch where Tony had poured his first load of water was now dry.

This is ridiculous, he thought, and straightened up to look along the high-water mark for anything large that might be used as a water container. *But I could waste ages looking and still not find anything.* He reached out to touch the whale, more confidently this time, and stroked it.

"Poor old thing," he said out loud, then turned and ran back to the water. He began to get into a rhythm—bending to force the bag into the sea; walking quickly but stiffly over the sand to the whale with his arm held out awkwardly sideways so that the bag of water didn't bump against his legs; pouring the water, not too quickly, over a different part of the whale's body; giving the whale a pat; then running back to the sea again.

He talked as he worked, disjointed phrases that kept him in contact with the inert creature on the sand—"I'm coming . . . there you are . . . poor old thing . . . back in a minute . . . that's too much, I'll tip some out . . . here I come." The more he talked, and the more he patted the whale, the less it seemed to squeak, as though it were listening to him. When he stroked the flank, it quivered. "Dear old thing," he whispered.

The sun was beginning to warm the air, and he became unpleasantly hot with the exertion. He threw down the bag, stripped off his sweater and shirt, and ran to the pile of shells with them. The ends of his sweater sleeves were sodden with salt water from their repeated dipping in the sea. He squeezed them out, making a dark patch on the sand, surrounded by dark dents with tiny rims, like moon craters, where the drops had fallen.

"Brilliant!" he shouted, as he turned back toward the sea, still holding the clothes. He raced down to the water and pushed them in, moving the sweater about until the wool was saturated and heavy. Bundling shirt and sweater together, he ran back to the whale and spread them over the top of its head, leaving the blowhole clear.

"Here you are. How's that for a great idea!"

The routine with the bag began again. Generally the whale lay motionless, but once when Tony was sluicing its side, it arched its back, and its great tail rose slowly, remained poised in the air for a few seconds, then was slowly lowered again. Next time Tony returned with water, he poured it over the tail, watching the water cascade off the edges and wishing he had enough sweaters to cover the whole whale. The back margin of the tail was notched and scarred in one place.

Perhaps something attacked it, he thought.

He occasionally replenished the water in the sweater and shirt, but they needed less attention than the larger area of exposed skin. He was tiring rapidly.

"Howard's been a long time," he said. "As soon as he comes with some help, we'll get you back into the sea." He looked deep into the eye again. "It's funny—I feel as though you're talking to me, even though you're not saying anything."

On his next trip with water in the bag, one of the handles broke, and in clutching at the collapsing bag, he punctured it with one of his fingers. All the contents were wasted on the sand, and he had to turn back. Now he had to hold the remaining handle with one hand and use his other hand to hold closed the hole he had accidentally made. Keeping his hands in these positions, he could get only a pathetically small quantity of water into the bag, shuffle over to the whale with it, and dribble it out over the skin. Not more than a couple of cupfuls each time.

Unable to go on much longer, he was greatly relieved when he saw a four-wheel-drive truck approaching along the sand. It stopped a few yards from the whale. Howard and two others climbed out of the cab, and several men jumped off the back. They had brought buckets with them, and two of the men went straight to the sea to fetch water.

"Good lad," said Howard. "Still alive, is it? You have a bit of a rest now while we set about rolling it back into the sea. Best move these clothes before they get trampled on." He threw them into the cab of the truck, then briskly organized the men so that he and five others stood alongside the whale, while two still plied the buckets of water.

CHAPTER

2

~~~~~~~~~~

HOWARD CALLED "READY," and the six men placed their hands on the whale, all standing along one side of its great body. They braced themselves. "Now!" called Howard, and they all pushed together. The whale rolled slightly, but then sank back into its original position.

"Okay," said Howard, "now we know what it feels like. Don't let it drop back next time. Josh, go around and keep his flipper tucked in, will you? Ready. Now!"

They strained again and held their positions so that the whale stayed in its new position.

"Ready. Now!"

The whale started to thrash about, making their task more difficult.

"Easy now, easy. Ready. Now!"

Refreshed after his brief rest, Tony joined them. He could feel the flesh shuddering under his hands.

"Ready. Now!"

The whale had now rolled half a complete turn from its original position and was now lying on its other side. The men straightened up for a moment. Howard looked along the beach.

"They've come, then," he said quietly.

The others looked in the same direction. About fifty yards along the beach, a whale lay on its side in the shallow water. The waves lapped around it, but was firmly stranded on the sand. Just beyond it lay two more dark shapes. In deeper water another whale was swimming steadily on the surface, heading for the beach. A small gasp of spray came from its blowhole as a wave buffeted it. Two of the men ran across and waded into the water in front of it, shouting and splashing in an effort to make it turn back. It slewed around in a fast, banking U-turn, but the waves caught it broadside on and pushed it inexorably onward until it grounded.

"Why have they come?" asked Tony.

"They've come to help this one," answered Howard. "It's been making distress calls."

"How can they help?"

"They can't, that's the trouble. They just get stranded on the beach like this one. We're going to need a lot more help."

"I'll go," said Josh. "Do I need to bring anything apart from people and buckets?"

"Look, I don't know," said Howard. "That's the trouble. Now that there are five of them, it all looks hopeless, but we've got to give it a go. The Wildlife man'll tell us what to do when he gets here. Look, Josh, just get everyone you can. Everyone in the place. They can all take turns pushing."

As Josh drove away, Howard turned back to the whale.

"The question is, do we keep going with this one, or do we try to help one of the new ones? Old Number One here has been high and dry for longest. Maybe the new ones stand a better chance of surviving."

"But he hasn't been dry," protested Tony. "Not for long, anyway. I kept him as wet as I could."

"I know you did, and you did really well. I just don't know what to do for the best, that's all. At least we ought to go and have a look at the others, anyway."

"Well, can I borrow a bucket, then, to keep Number One wet?"

"Sure." Howard and the six others trudged off over the sand toward the four new whales that were stranded.

Tony took the bucket to the water's edge, wishing he had asked for two, so that their weights would have balanced while he was carrying them full. Never mind, one bucket was better than a torn plastic bag anyway. Pulled over to one side by the loaded bucket, he staggered back to the whale. As he poured the water gently over the whale's head, he remembered that his sweater and shirt were in the cab with Josh. Darn! They could have been useful for keeping the whale damp, as before.

If Josh managed to find other men to come and help, there might soon be people milling about all over the beach. He had better move his shells before they were trampled underfoot. The plastic bag was nowhere to be seen; it had probably blown away in the strong breeze.

He turned the nautilus upside down and put some of the smaller shells inside it. Carrying the larger ones loose in one hand and the filled nautilus in the other, he was able to carry all his shells at once up the beach to the ridge of dry dunes. There he found a substantial clump of marram at the summit of one of the dunes and rested his collection in the middle of it. Nobody would step on it there. If anybody walked over the dunes, they would keep to the depressions of sand between the tufts of grass. He broke off some blades of marram and placed them over the shells to conceal them. He couldn't break many because the harsh plant tore at the skin of his hands, and he had been away from the whale for quite long enough. He plunged down the dune in two giant, slithering strides and raced back to the whale.

"I'm back," he said, stroking the whale's head. The whale's mouth opened once, then shut. "Okay, I'll get some water," said Tony, starting his work with the bucket again. Although he had no clothes on above the waist, he was beginning to feel uncomfortably warm with the effort and uncomfortably aware that the warmth of the sun might soon be causing the whales a good deal of distress.

Having finished their inspection of the other whales, a couple of the men wandered back.

"So now we've got five whales," sighed Howard. "I wish I'd thought to ask Josh to bring some kind of covering for them now that the day's warming up. That wet sweater was a good idea of Tony's, and now we've lost even that. Let's just hope we get a lot more help really soon."

"What are the other whales like?" asked Tony.

This time, Graeme answered, "One of them's bigger than this one. Otherwise they all look pretty much the same. None of them seems to be hurt. I wonder if we shouldn't stop trying to move any of them and just work at keeping all the whales wet until we get some help."

"I hope to goodness Josh is bringing plenty more people," grunted Howard.

"Here he is," shouted Tony, seeing first one, then a second and third truck.

As the trucks started down off the track and onto the beach, Tony could see people running behind them. People with buckets. People with bundles. Tony turned and looked the other way. Two people were running along from the direction of his home.

"Mom and Dad," he said, "and they've got a bucket. Somebody must have phoned them."

Josh drove up in the leading truck, which had men hanging on all over the back like ticks on a steer. They jumped down and started unloading spades, ropes, and sacking. The other two trucks stopped farther back, and Tony could see more gear being dumped on the sand. Soon each whale was covered with wet sacking, its blowhole left clear. The people who had come on foot began to arrive. They were mainly women and children, and most carried buckets.

There must have been sixty people on the beach. There couldn't be many left at home, thought Tony.

"Hello, love," panted his mom as she hung on to his shoulder and bent over, trying to get her breath back. "I've brought you another shirt and a couple of muffins and some lemonade but you'll have to drink it out of the bottle because I forgot to bring a cup."

"Thanks, Mom, but we can't stop to eat just now. Anyway, I'm not hungry," he said, and suddenly was.

"You carry on," said Howard. "We're going to stop for a couple of minutes anyway, now that everyone's arrived, so that we can discuss a plan of action."

He called Josh and one or two of the others, and they stood talking near the truck.

"Here," said Mom, handing Tony a muffin.

"Okay, then, thanks. Come and see Number One."

The whale lay motionless, swathed in damp sacking.

"Don't go too near," warned Dad. "However good-natured animals are, they can be very unpredictable when they're alarmed or hurt, and that one's big enough to be downright dangerous."

"I think he's safe, though," Tony said. "I've kept away from his mouth, and I've been careful of his tail. It thrashes about a bit sometimes, but I'm sure he wouldn't mean to hurt anyone."

"I'm not saying he would, but if you get crippled by that thing rolling on you, it'll be no comfort to know that he didn't mean it."

"Don't," said Mom, "you're giving me the heebie-jeebies. Put your shirt on, Tony, before your back gets burned."

"How did you know about my clothes being wet?"

"Josh left them at his house with Sue while he went around telling people about the whales. Sue phoned to tell us where you were. She's going to rinse the sweater for me. It'll be a wonder if it isn't a write-off, with all that salt and grit in the wool. Hours it took me to make, too."

"I'm sorry, Mom, I didn't realize. I just had to use it for the whale."

"All right, love, I'm glad you did really, I suppose."

Tony finished the muffins and drank all the lemonade. He told them about finding the paper nautilus. It was difficult to believe he had found it that same morning—it seemed more like days ago. Dad filled a couple of buckets and sluiced the parts of the whale that weren't covered by the sacking.

15

"See what I mean?" he said, as the great tail rose and fell again. "He could break your neck, no sweat."

Howard was calling everyone on the beach to gather together in one place. There were more than forty men, half as many children, and nine women. Tony knew them all by sight at least, and he saw the children practically every day. In a place like this, strangers were a rarity. David and Sam came across to him. Sam had some chewing gum in his pocket, and they each had a piece.

Howard started speaking in a rush, not looking at the crowd but gazing slightly to one side and out to sea.

He's nervous, thought Tony. *How strange. After all, he knows everybody.*

Gradually, though, Howard seemed to get used to being looked at by so many people, and he relaxed. He told them that when he had first run to take his dog home and get help, he had telephoned the Fisheries and Wildlife officer in Seaton.

"He said he'd come and give us a hand, but he's fifty miles away, so it'll take a bit of time. I expect him soon, though. Of course, when I phoned him, there was only one whale on the beach, but he won't be surprised to find that there are more. When a whale strands, it often sends out distress calls to the other whales in its group. Some of them are quite likely to follow it in, which is what these four did. There's still the danger that more will come—we must try to get this lot back into the sea before that happens. We'll have teams of seven or eight men to each whale, to roll them back into the sea.

"Two of the ladies, stand on the dunes and keep a watch for more whales; Mr. Russell, the Wildlife fellow, wants details of numbers and times of arrival. You can start by noting down the estimated times of arrival of these five. Tony and Graeme can help you there. There's a pencil in the glove compartment of my truck, and you'll have to write in the margin of the service manual unless someone's got some paper.

"You kids can take buckets and keep the whales wet—

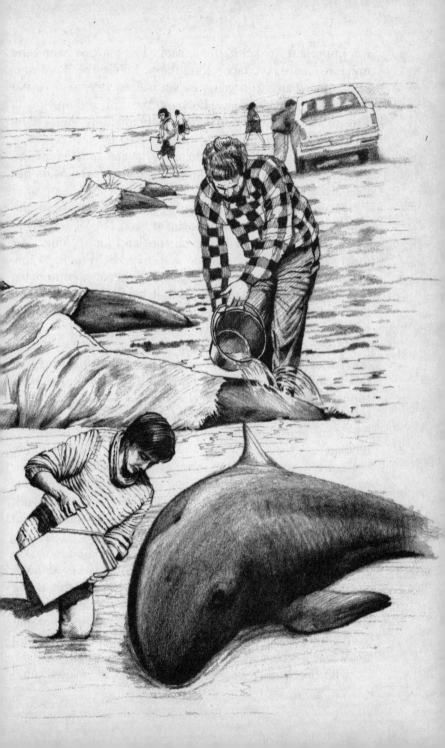

it's important to keep them cool. The sacking won't be much use once we start rolling them. Looks like about four kids to a whale. You can sort yourselves into groups. No water in the blowholes. Lots on the tail and fins, Mr. Russell says. And we must comfort them all the time—they must be very frightened.

"You other ladies can stand by to act as messengers, either between groups working on different whales or between the beach and home.

"Mrs. Russell says when the whales are back in the water, they won't be able to swim at first. They'll get sort of cramps, I think, after being out on land for so long. We must keep them in the shallow water and help them to stay upright until they can manage on their own, otherwise they might drown. And we mustn't let them go too early, or they'll just restrand; hold on to them once they're in the water.

"Okay, let's get started, then. Oh, I forgot to say, we don't want anybody hurt. I don't know how dangerous it is doing this—it obviously depends a lot on how cooperative the whales are. We're going to have our work cut out as it is, so the last thing we want is having to cope with someone who's got himself rolled on. Just take care, that's all. Right, let's go."

Tony went back to Number One, and David and Sam came with him. They were joined by Katie, David's cousin. Sam gave her a piece of chewing gum, and they set to work with the buckets. Tony had to stop while his mom made notes on the arrival of the whales.

"I don't know," he said. "I left home soon after six, so by the time I'd found the shells and got this far, it must have been about half past seven. He was still a bit damp then, so I don't suppose he'd been here long, though I didn't see him arrive because I was looking down at the sand all the time. The other whales arrived later—Graeme's got a watch—he may have noticed what time that was."

The beach was noisy now, with shouts of "Watch out!"

"Heave!" "Ready, now!" "Over here a bit, can you?" and "Wait!" In fact, Graeme broke off to go around to each group and suggest that they should be quieter so that the whales weren't unnecessarily alarmed. Each of the five stranded whales was the center of a hive of activity.

Except for Tony's mom and Mrs. Hawsworth, who went to stand on the dunes watching for more whales, all the women had joined in with the pushing and rolling. More children had arrived from the village, some with buckets, and two of the bucket gangs had organized themselves into chains, passing the buckets from hand to hand. People had lined up alongside the whales and were gradually maneuvering them back toward the sea. At first the whales thrashed about a bit, but they gradually stopped and even seemed to cooperate, summoning up their energy to roll with the impetus given them by the straining people.

The whale that had arrived last and had been furthest down the beach was soon virtually afloat, and lay almost motionless on the water, rising and tilting slightly with the swell but making no movements of its own except for the quivering dilations and contractions of its blowhole. People stationed themselves thigh or waist deep along each side of it, patting and stroking it. A couple of the men were wearing wetsuits, but the rest wore ordinary clothes. The water tugged at sodden corduroys and denims and seeped along the sleeves of shirts.

"We could all do with wetsuits," said Josh. "This could be a long business."

Katie's mom was sent up to the houses in one of the trucks to collect wetsuits for anyone who owned one. Her sister, David's mom, went with her with a list of instructions. Some of the wetsuits were in houses whose inhabitants were all now on the beach. In each different pocket of her jeans she had a front-door key and a crumpled scrap of paper—"Graeme, box in garage" . . . "Les, cupboard under stairs, green bag" . . . "Jeff, car trunk."

Number One, who had been furthest up the beach, was

next to last back into the water. Each time he rested on his belly in the shallow water, he was given the time to breathe before being pushed over again. Finally he, too, was afloat. The largest whale had not yet been returned to the sea, since the original team of people had been unable to roll her without help. Work on her began once the other four were afloat.

"What do we do now?" asked Sam.

"I dunno," said Graeme. "None of them really looks ready to take off just yet. In fact they look pretty sick to me. I reckon so long as they'll just lie still in the water like that, we'll keep them steady and wait for Mr. Russell from the Wildlife to turn up. He should be here any—"

A woman's voice yelled something from a long way away. Then there were two. Tony's mom and Mrs. Hawsworth, two small gray shapes against the sheet-metal sky over the dunes, were shouting and waving and pointing. Their words were lost in the distance, but their meaning was clear— through the gentle waves offshore, dark shapes were bearing down on the beach. Seven. No, eleven. Twelve. Goodness knows how many whales, swimming purposefully toward the sand.

Anybody not actually involved in looking after the four whales in the shallows raced back along the beach to face the oncoming group. "No!" they yelled, "go back, go back!"

They waded into the water and slashed at it with the buckets to make great smacking noises. Number One, under Tony's hand, began to tremble. They slapped the surface with their hands and worked the water into a brown, gritty turbulence in their frenzy. "Go away, go back!"

Some of the great shapes came driving on, oblivious of the puny efforts from the wall of people facing them, and their bellies ground into the sand. Others banked into a turn, as if to make out to sea again, and were caught broadside by the waves and pushed ashore.

They lay with the water gently lapping around them.

The wet mounds of their flanks shone sleekly in the sun, and they lay at peace. A cormorant flew overhead along the shore, then veered and made out to sea. The stillness was complete.

"Oh, God," said Howard.

CHAPTER

3

~~~~~~~~~~

JIM RUSSELL, the Fisheries and Wildlife Officer, arrived in a Land Rover with a coat of arms on the door.

"False killer whales," he said. "Last I heard, there was only one—when did the others arrive?"

"There was a batch of four fairly soon afterward, then this lot have only just got here," answered Josh. "Those two women up on the dunes have been noting the times. The five whales over there with the people standing by them are the first five that we rolled back down the beach. We're keeping them away from the beach, but we don't know what else to do."

"I see you've used sacking to keep them wet, but what have you used those spades and ropes for?"

"Nothing yet. I just grabbed some when I was up by the houses fetching more people. I thought we might use the spades for digging or leverage or something, and I thought we might tie a rope around each whale's tail and drag it along over the sand, but I don't think it would have worked, somehow."

"No, you'd have injured the whales. It's better just to roll them. You could use the spades, though—dig a depression near each new stranded whale and it'll fill with water and make the bucket work easier. Then hurry to get each one off its side and onto its belly. If they've lain on their sides too long, it upsets their sense of balance once they're back in the water."

Mr. Russell changed into a wetsuit in his Land Rover

and went to inspect the whales more closely. As the tide slowly receded, the newest arrivals were becoming more exposed. There were fourteen of them, including two quite small ones. People were already standing by them, sluicing them with bucketfuls of water.

The five original whales were lying in the shallows. All the whales made occasional squeaking, chirping noises. Tony stood close to Number One, talking to him. He no longer felt self-conscious about talking to a whale—he'd noticed that it seemed to come naturally to people. Sam, in particular, had had quite a long conversation with Number One, though he had now abandoned him in favor of one of the newer arrivals. Tony could never do that—Number One was *his* whale.

Mr. Russell came over.

"These four don't look too bad. I think we might try getting them away now." He looked closely at Number One. "Take him a bit deeper and let go of his flipper a minute," he said to Tony and Graeme. Number One slowly slid over sideways and came to rest when a flipper touched the sand. They quickly righted him. "No, this one looks pretty sick to me."

"He was out of the water longest," said Graeme, "and he got pretty dry."

"Okay, let's leave him here for a bit," said Mr. Russell. "Looks as though he might not make it. We can't hope to save them all anyway."

He moved away to discuss the next step with Howard and Josh.

Graeme saw the expression on Tony's face and looked away.

"Don't worry, we won't give up before we really have to. Best for him not to go with the others just yet, though."

"I'm sorry," said Tony, "he's sort of special."

"Of course he is. Just try not to get too involved with him, though, just in case."

Tony thought of his first meeting with the whale early

that morning, of the depths of the eye into which he had gazed. He quickly rubbed his eyes and watched with exaggerated interest as the measurements of the other four whales were noted and they were gently escorted into deeper water. They began to move freely as the depth of the water increased, and were able to propel themselves gracefully away when the people accompanying them had reached waist depth. The four glided silently out to sea and were lost to view. There were cheers from the beach. Four gone, fifteen to go. Tony looked out over the great expanse of water and imagined them surging back to the freedom of their natural environment.

"We'll just have to hope for the best," said Mr. Russell.

There was a shout from the dunes. Mom and Mrs. Hawsworth, jumping and yelling and making long sweeping movements with their arms. More whales coming in?

Katie ran to the base of the dunes and came panting back. "They're going sideways. Those four. The current's taking them. They're being swept toward the Head."

The dunes were soon thick with people watching helplessly as the four whales were carried inexorably toward the rocky outcrops, which jutted into the sea from the headland. Graeme and Tony, steadying Number One, were the only people down by the water's edge. The other fourteen whales lay temporarily abandoned, shrouded in wet sacking. There was a hubbub on the dunes as people craned to see, those who had binoculars keeping up a running commentary. Then there was quiet as they drifted down onto the beach again. Katie ran to Tony and Graeme.

"They're on the rocks. All four of them. Mr. Russell's going to have a look."

The Land Rover moved off along the beach with several passengers. A few people picked up buckets and returned to the fourteen stranded whales, dampening the sacking and sluicing the exposed skin. The rest stood around disconsolately in small groups.

"Go and have a rest," said Graeme. "I'll give a shout if I need help."

Tony waded out of the water and lay on his back on the sand. His wet clothes clung to him uncomfortably, and he began to feel cold. Dad came and sat beside him and spread a bit of dry sacking over him to keep the wind off.

"Thanks." Tony felt ready for bed, although it was only midday. He closed his eyes. He could hear the whisper of the sand as Dad ran rivulets of it through his fingers. The sea sounded strangely remote and otherworldly. Tony drifted on the edge of sleep. His consciousness rose and fell, like a whale moving gently with the ebb and flow of the shallow water.

The Land Rover returned, and Tony watched his father join the group of people who gathered around Mr. Russell. He looked down toward Graeme.

"Is he still all right?" he called.

"Yes, he's okay. Have a rest while you can."

After a while, Dad came back and sat down with a sigh. Tony cleared the sleep from his head and sat up, holding the sacking around his damp shoulders.

"They're washed up on the rocks," said Dad, "and have been a bit battered in the process. One of them's got a bad gash on one of its flippers. It's going to be difficult getting them off again. A couple of guys have stayed there to keep them wet. We may just have to forget about them for a bit and concentrate on the fifteen left here. Jim Russell thinks the same thing may happen to any others that we get back into the sea from the beach. They'll be so weak and disoriented when they first swim off that the current's likely to take them as well and dump them all on the rocks. Howard's come up with some crazy scheme to take them to the harbor and launch them from there. The water's calm in the harbor and there's no strong current across the entrance when they reach the open sea."

"How do you mean, take them to the harbor? That's around the headland."

"Take them overland."

"What?" Tony was wide awake. "What do you mean? How?"

"One by one on the back of a four-wheel drive. There shouldn't be any problem once they're on. It'll be getting them on and off without hurting them that'll be the difficult bit."

"I must tell Graeme. He hasn't heard any of this."

Tony waded back into the water alongside Number One. Graeme listened incredulously.

"Good for Howard," he said. "He'll do it, if anyone can. Look, I must go and help. See if you can get two or three of the women to give you a hand looking after this one—

people with wetsuits if you can—it's a bit drafty standing about in the water when you're soaked to the skin, isn't it."

Tony waded out again and ran over to the four-wheel drives, where most of the people were now gathered. Although several were now wearing wetsuits, most of these were men and would be needed for lifting the whales. Carol from the milk bar was wearing one, though, and she pointed out her friend Tracey, also in a wetsuit, who was on bucket duty near one of the whales.

"That's fine by me," said Tracey. "I was getting too darned hot running about up to my neck in rubber."

The three of them took over from Graeme, who went to join Howard and Jim Russell by the trucks. Number One lazed in the water, his belly just clear of the sand. His tail and flippers moved occasionally as he maintained his equilibrium. Tony and the two girls had little to do, but Tony was glad of the moral support. If Number One rolled over and his blowhole was submerged, Tony wouldn't be able to right the whale unaided. Occasionally the current tugged at their legs, and they steadied themselves against the whale. The four of them were conspicuously inactive compared with the bustle elsewhere on the beach.

Teams of people were forming around three of the whales, and the three trucks had been positioned nearby, each with its back toward the head of a whale and about half a whale's length away.

Along the path over the dunes from the houses five women were staggering, laden as though they had just come from a supermarket. They heaved their tote bags onto the back of one of the trucks and started to pass around the contents.

"Food," said Tracey. "Oh boy, am I starving, and we're stuck here. Shall I give them a shout and ask them to bring us something?"

"Don't you dare," said Carol. "What would everyone think, us standing here yelling for food!"

"What I'd really like," said Tracey, "is some bacon and a couple of sausages. I didn't have any breakfast before coming down here. When they came around to get my dad's wetsuit, I just put mine on and came straight down to see what was going on. I didn't think I'd be here all that long." There was a gurgling noise. "Oh, heck, was that my stomach, or was it the whale's?"

David and Sam came running toward them, David carrying an interestingly full bread wrapper.

"Brought you some stuff," he said. "Some sandwiches and some cookies. The coffee's all gone, but Mrs. Clifton's gone to make some more. They've spread a tarpaulin out beside one of the smaller whales, and they're going to try to lift it onto the truck with that."

They passed the bread bag around, and all five of them ate hungrily. Some of the sandwiches had fallen apart, and there were slices of cheese among the cookie crumbs.

Along the beach, there was a low chant of "Ready, heave . . . ready, heave!" A seething mass of people was bunched over one of the whales like an elongated rugby scrum. David and Sam ran off to watch.

"We'll come back later and let you know how it's going," called David.

Suddenly Tony wanted to pee. Oh no! His shirt had dried on his back in the wind, but his trousers were still sodden to the top. He wondered if he could pee in the water without the girls noticing and decided he couldn't risk it. Somewhere up in the dunes, then. But that meant leaving Number One with the two girls. Would they look after him properly? Suppose the whale started to drown and they couldn't keep his blowhole above the surface? He'd better wait until Sam and David came back, then he could leave all four of them on duty. Darn.

The chanting went on. "Ready, heave . . . ready, heave!" The knot of people, still hunched over, didn't appear to have moved.

"They've got to do this fifteen times," he thought. "It's going to take all afternoon."

And what about the four whales bleeding on the rocks? They had been left there while all activity was concentrated on the beach. And what if there were more whales still out at sea, waiting to send another batch in to strand themselves?

We must hurry, he thought. Then I *must hurry. Can't wait for David and Sam*.

"I'm just going up to the dunes to check whether Mom needs anything," he said to the girls as nonchalantly as he could, and turned and started wading out without waiting for their response. He walked casually up the beach, as if toward his mother and Mrs. Hawsworth, still standing sentinel against the sky, but he veered away in the last fifty yards and ran frantically into a secluded gully between two dunes.

The crisis past, he was now desperate to get back to Number One lest the girls should fail in some way while he was gone. He gave up all pretense of going to see the two women and hurried back to the whale. His whale. Everything was just as he had left it. He and the two girls studiously avoided commenting on his brief absence.

"Is he still all right?"

"Yes, if you ask me, he's feeling fine. He seems to be keeping his balance okay."

"Trouble is, the journey overland to the harbor'll probably set him back again, and we shall have to go through all this business again over there—getting him used to the water and everything."

There had been a lull in the activity around the other whales, but now came a sudden shout—"Heave!"—and the knot of people lifted the tarpaulin and hoisted the head end of the whale onto the back of the four-wheel drive. Six men crouched on the truck, holding its head and front flippers. Its tail and much of its sleek, tapering body remained unsupported by the vehicle and lay cradled in the tarpaulin, which was held at waist height by a team of people standing on the sand. Tony could see Sam and Katie among the bucket squad, dousing the whale and half the people as well, in arcing sheets of seawater. The whale's great spine arched slowly, bearing the tail aloft.

"Now!" shouted someone. "Do it now!"

"Ready," came another voice. "Heave!"

The men on the truck and those on the sand all heaved together on the tarpaulin, and it carried the whale's bulk forward until its head rested near the cab of the truck and its tail protruded diagonally over the end. The six men remained crouched beside it. The door of the cab slammed, and the engine whirred briefly. Then there was silence. The engine whirred again and retched.

"Brilliant," said Tracey. "Now someone'll have to go and phone for a two truck and say, 'Please come and give us a tow, and by the way we've got a dirty great whale on the truck.'"

Again the engine gave a heaving, empty cough, but

this time there was a tantalizing splutter of life just before it died.

"Next time," muttered Carol.

And, sure enough, there was a sudden throbbing current of sound. Strangely it seemed to galvanize the people rather than the truck. The truck remained static, but the people, who had been standing tense and rigid, were set in motion again. Buckets of water were passed up to the six who crouched with the whale, several men positioned themselves around the back of the truck where the blade of the tail projected and the end of the tarpaulin dangled, and onlookers stood back from the front of the truck, to clear a way up and along the beach toward the track to the houses.

Slowly the truck started forward over the sand and progressed at walking pace to the gap in the dunes where the track cut through. About fifteen men walked alongside and behind it, two of them supporting the tail. In their wake went most of the younger children from the beach.

Looks like a state funeral, thought Tony and immediately wished he hadn't. He looked quickly at Number One and found that the eye was looking back at him. *No funeral for you, my friend*, he thought, *not if I can help it*.

The truck bearing the whale passed through the gap in the dunes and was gone. The handful of faithful souls who had remained on bucket duty keeping the other thirteen whales wet were rejoined by those who had stopped work to watch the departure of the first. Tarpaulins were spread on the sand in front of two more of the whales, and two more rugby scrums formed.

David ambled over to Tony and the girls.

"How about that?" he said. "What if they hadn't been able to start the engine! Sam's gone to watch them getting the whale off and into the harbor at the other end, then he reckons he'll cadge a lift back on the empty truck."

"There won't be room, surely. There must have been twenty or more men altogether."

"No, most of those'll stay over by the harbor, ready to

lift the next whale off. Only seven are supposed to come back—eight counting the driver. That way, there should be enough people working in each place, plus about seven to look after each whale during the journey. Why don't you come and watch? There doesn't seem to be much to do here."

"There isn't, but there might be," said Tony. "I don't know how much longer Number One's just going to mooch about like this. Suppose he tries to swim into deeper water, then gets a cramp and starts to drown?"

"If he does, I don't know whether we'll be able to save him, even with all three of us here," said Carol. "You saw it took about twenty-five of them to lift that one just now. I know we'd have his buoyancy in the water to help us, but we'd be having to hold him up for a length of time, not just for a moment."

"Then we could shout for help," said Tony. "Anyway, I feel better staying here. I'm going to stick with Number One now that I've gotten to know him and he's gotten to know me."

By now there were two separate, asynchronous chants, one of "Ready, now!", the other of "Right, heave!" as the next two whales were being rolled onto their respective tarpaulins. David ran back to watch. There was a triumphant shout as one of the whales was raised onto the back of the waiting truck. The truck moved off at a walking pace. This time, there were only four men sitting on the back with the whale, holding buckets of water, and one walking behind holding the tail.

The other whale was one of the largest. It was lifted to the level of the truck's waiting back, but the men straining to hold it high didn't have the extra strength to swing it on and forward.

"Down! Down again!" someone called. Tony heard their grunts of relief as the whale, in its tarpaulin hammock, was set back on the sand again. More people came to help. Wherever there was a space an extra pair of hands grabbed the edge of the tarpaulin. The scrum was silent, waiting, breathing.

"Ready, now!"

The scrum rose erect bearing its huge burden, staggered, then lunged forward so that the whale's head and front edge of the tarpaulin rested on the truck. Men on the back of the truck reached down and scrabbled for the edges of tarpaulin, and the whale was maneuvered on in a series of ungainly, shuffling slithers. The tail still projected a long way over at the back; ropes tied to the tarpaulin were passed back under the tail and up and over to the top of the cab, so that much of the weight of the tail was now supported.

There was a pause and a discussion. Then Tony saw the ropes being slackened off again for a moment while sacking was wound around them so that they wouldn't cut into the whale's flesh. The ropes were secured again, and the truck moved off.

Three whales gone overland!

Soon the first truck came back and a handful of men jumped down. Sam wasn't there. In fact, none of the children who had followed it had returned with it.

Must be pretty interesting over at the harbor, thought Tony, and half wished he could go and watch instead of being stuck in one spot.

"I've got to sit down for a minute," said Tracey. "I must have been bending over slightly toward the whale all the time. My back's killing me." She lurched out of the water, wincing. "Holy mackerel, the hunchback of Notre Dame." She lay on the sand. "Wake me up when it's teatime."

CHAPTER

4

~~~~~~~~~~

ANOTHER WHALE WAS IN POSITION on the back of the first four-wheel drive by the time the second truck returned empty.

"I should think they'll leave this one till last," said Carol. "It's probably a lot more comfortable than the ones lying on the sand."

Jim Russell and Howard were crossing the sand toward them. Howard's curly hair, sticky with salt, stood out wildly around his head, and his eyes were red-rimmed from the sharp wind. Tracey opened one eye and squinted at them against the bright light.

"We're checking on all the whales," said Howard. "Jim's just off to look at the ones on the rocks, and we want to see how this one's doing."

Tracey joined them.

"He's fine."

"He looks a bit lethargic to me."

"He must be keeping himself in this position, mustn't he?" said Carol. "I mean, if he were completely unconscious, he'd be drifting about far more than he is, and he'd be bumping into our legs every time there was a movement in the water. He must have made the decision to stay here for the moment. We wouldn't be able to keep him here if he didn't want to stay."

"Well, he's better than some of them," said Howard. "Two of them back there are dead."

"No! How?"

"Just exposure and shock, I expect," said Jim. "Or maybe they weren't well in the first place and that's why they stranded. We hope to get hold of a vet eventually to come and have a look at them and see if he can see what might have been wrong with them. Trouble is, it's difficult to find anyone on a Sunday. Mr. Gibson's the nearest, and he's been called out to a mare who's having twins—she's lost one already and looks like losing the other one too. Anyway, it looks as though we'd better carry on shifting all the other whales and have another look at this one nearer the end. I'm just off to the rocks. See you later."

Howard waited until Jim was out of earshot.

"It's his first stranding. He's heard about them from other Wildlife officers, but it's a bit different having to deal with it yourself. His main interest is waterfowl, apparently. We're all just doing the best we can."

"It was a great idea to move them overland. How's it going over at the harbor?"

"Fine. Once they're in the water, they're keeping pretty still, like this one. We've collected a few more helpers on our way through the town."

"All the kids seem to have stayed over at the harbor."

"That's because we didn't give them a ride back on the four-wheel drive. We didn't want this whole thing developing into a joyride for the kids, with them swarming around the trucks and jumping on and off the back—that way someone's going to get killed. We need to be able to concentrate on what we're doing, manhandling animals of this size. There's plenty for the kids to watch, over at the harbor, with the unloading of the whales, and they can always walk back to the beach when they feel like it."

"What's it like driving along the road with a whale on the truck?"

"Crazy. Some of the motorists—you should see the expression on their faces! We had one twit trying to overtake us at a narrow part—nearly had everyone in the ditch. Mostly, though, they've been pretty sensible. One guy, he stopped and asked us what it was all about, and he's gone home for his camera and he's coming to join us when he's phoned some people in a group called the Friends of the Whales."

"Who are they?"

"I don't really know. He says they're specially interested in whale strandings and might give us some advice."

"But we're doing all right, aren't we?"

"I dunno, pal, I really don't. Maybe it was our fault, those four going onto the rocks. Maybe we shouldn't have sent them off so soon. Of course, we've no way of knowing whether the ones in the harbor are going to manage any better. The whole thing may just be a waste of time and effort. There goes another one, look."

A truck was moving off slowly, bearing its precious cargo.

"Your mom's down on the beach now, trying to get all the times and measurements and things in some sort of order. We reckoned she and Mrs. Hawsworth'd been stuck up in those dunes long enough, so Katie and her mom have taken over up there, keeping an eye open for more whales. We've measured all the whales on the beach and we're trying to keep a note of which is which and when each was moved to the harbor and so on. Jim says that's the sort of information that's always collected when there's a stranding. He wants to measure this one, too, while he's at it."

"This one's easy to identify—he's got a notch in the blade of his tail—see?"

Jim jogged up to them, out of breath and hot.

"These wetsuits are a mixed blessing; I was glad of mine on the rocks, but I'm sweating now."

"How are the ones on the rocks?"

"Not good. One of them was quite badly hurt when it was first thrown on, and one of the others is getting knocked about quite a bit, too, by the breakers. There are a couple of lads over there with buckets, trying to keep the whales damp all over. Although the water swirls around the whales' bellies sometimes, their backs and flippers are getting very dry. We're never going to get them off, and when the tide comes in, they're just going to be battered to death. I'm going to have to shoot them. It's for their own good."

"Can't we get them off somehow?"

"No way. Next thing, somebody'd get killed and I'd be held responsible. Whatever we do for any of these whales, we've got to put human life first. Now, let me just measure this one, then I'll go and get my gun."

He held the end of the measuring tape to the edge of the whale's tail blade and passed the rest of the tape to Howard, who unwound it until it reached the front of Number One's head.

"One hundred and forty-seven inches," said Howard.

"Not fully grown. And a chunk out of his fluke," said Jim, writing the information in a damp notebook. The edges of the pages were fluffy and stuck together.

"What's a fluke?" asked Tracey.

"The flat part of his tail—and the narrow bit just in front, that's the stock. Right, let's go."

"See you later," said Howard, and he and Jim trudged wearily up the beach toward the Land Rover.

The operation of removing the whales from the beach was continuing. Tony couldn't see clearly how many were still left, but there seemed to be seven, and two of those were dead. It would soon be Number One's turn to be moved. He stroked the whale's flank, then bent and gripped its flipper for a moment.

"Not long now." There was a moist snort from the blowhole.

Jim had collected his rifle and was heading back toward the rocks, while Howard had rejoined the whale-lifting teams.

Thank goodness Number One didn't go with the others and get swept onto the rocks, Tony thought, and held the flipper again.

The whale's head bumped gently against his legs. Was

that intentional? Had the whale given him a companionable nudge, or had it been knocked against him by the swell?

There was the sound of a shot—a dry, empty crack, which only lasted for a split second. In this open expanse of sea and sand there was no resonance. Two more followed, then a pause.

"Poor things," said Carol. "I hope the fourth doesn't understand what's happening."

The people on the beach had stopped work and were standing listening. At last the fourth shot came. Followed by another. Then silence. Tony suddenly had a sense of the vastness of the scene. On the seaward side the horizon was unbroken; a great curve of metallic gray—a boundary between two elements, yet not marking the limit of either of them. Beyond his vision, both water and air went on and on, curving around the earth. Really, his foothold on the earth was very precarious. One knew all about gravity, of course, but still it was a wonder one didn't break away from one's moorings and drift away into space.

There was another shot.

"Whatever can he be doing?"

"Perhaps he missed, the first couple of times," said Tracey.

"Don't be stupid. Perhaps some more have gotten stranded there."

"Maybe he's shooting at something else."

"Like what?"

"Well, I don't know, do I?"

Another shot. Then three more in quick succession.

"Good grief, what's he got over there? That's eleven so far."

"Ten," said Carol.

"He's being attacked by Indians."

"Shut up, will you?"

There were no more shots, and after a while they saw Jim's figure in the distance, walking back along the beach.

"That's that, then," said Tracey.

Work resumed around the remaining stranded whales. Jim took his rifle back to his Land Rover, but they were surprised to see him climb inside the cab and shut the door.

"Is he going or something?"

"Probably just tired out. It must be hard work lifting those whales, and then there's the worry about what to do next. You could see Howard was tired too."

Just as his name was mentioned, Howard left the busy groups of whale lifters and bucket carriers and walked over to the Land Rover. He stood beside the cab for a while, talking to Jim through the window, then walked away again, leaving Jim sitting in the cab.

"It's Carol's turn for a rest," said Tracey. "See if you can find us a drink, will you? I'm as dry as anything. Must be the salt in the air making me so thirsty."

Carol tottered through the shallower water, nearly losing her balance as she came out onto dry land.

"My skin's gone all white and puffy in the water," she called. "My feet look like a corpse. We'd better take it in turns to come out more often, or we'll start rotting away."

Tony had sneakers on, so he wasn't sure about the state of his feet. They were certainly very cold. He tried waggling his toes, and they moved slowly and laboriously, like a slow-motion nightmare. A sheet of bright green seaweed floated past his knees then surged back again as the current caught it.

"We'll start growing barnacles soon," he said.

"Some whales have barnacles growing on them," said Tracey.

"How did you know that?"

"I can't remember, I saw it somewhere."

Carol returned with a plastic bottle full of water.

"They brought drinks back with them on one of their return trips from the harbor. D'you know it's after three o'clock?"

Only nine hours since Tony had left the house that

morning, but it seemed three times as long. They took turns drinking out of the bottle, then Carol took the empty bottle and lay on the sand for a while.

"It'll be a relief when we can get moving with this whale, won't it?" she said. "Here you are, Tony. You take the bottle back, it'll give you some exercise. I'll come back into the water." She waded in. "My feet are getting tired of all this wetness. Don't worry, we'll look after your whale for you."

"Yes, I know. Thanks. I just don't like to leave him, that's all."

He walked bandy-legged like a cowboy, but even so the stiff, salty wetness of his trousers chafed the insides of his legs. The thick cloth dragged with each step he took. Mom came to meet him.

"You could do with shorts. Dad said he was going to fetch you some, but he's gotten so involved in lifting whales, it must have slipped his mind. You'd better go home and get some."

"I'd never get that far, walking like this. It'd take all the skin off my legs."

"You don't have to wear your trousers all the way home—take them off when you're a couple of hundred yards along the beach, nobody'll see."

He was aghast. "I can't do that. Somebody'd be bound to see. Besides, I've got to get back to Number One. They might decide to move him soon."

"Well, I'll go, then. There's not a lot for me to do here at the moment. No new whales to record, thank goodness."

"Thanks, Mom."

He put the empty water bottle with several others on the sand and went to look at the remaining whales. There were five, but one was in position on its tarpaulin and was about to be hoisted onto the back of one of the trucks. The bucket squad thoroughly sluiced it with water, then stood back. People took up their positions along each side of the tarpaulin—about twelve people along each side.

At the call of "Ready!" they crouched ready to take the strain.

"Lift!"

They straightened up, gasping, with the sinews of their necks standing in ridges. Tony watched the effort involved as they swung the whale onto the truck. *They can't do this much more,* he thought.

Another whale was being rolled onto its tarpaulin. A third waited, attended only by its bucket squad. It lay festooned in damp sacking, right to the end of its flippers and tail. Only its blowhole and the front of its head were visible.

The two remaining whales were no longer black. They were a dry gray, encrusted and mottled with sand. One had a large blister on its flank, with a red wound underneath, and flies were beginning to congregate around the rim.

"Time to cover these up," said Jim Russell, who had come to stand beside Tony. He dumped some sacking on the sand and sorted out a piece, handing an end to Tony. They spread it over part of one of the dead whales, tucking the sides under and pushing sand against them to hold them down.

"How did this happen?" asked Tony, pointing to the gash.

"It's drying out and cracking; that sometimes happens when they've died. That's why I want to cover them up. I don't want people getting too upset; there are little kids around."

Tony remembered Howard's warning (it seemed days ago)—"He could die and crack open, poor old beggar"—and his eyes pricked as he thought of Number One. He must get back to him. He hurried to finish helping with the sacking shrouds.

"Why were there so many shots over by the rocks? What were you shooting at?"

There was a long silence. Tony thought maybe he hadn't heard. Jim was looking out to sea.

"What were you firing at?"

Jim cleared his throat. "One of the whales."

"But there were ten shots."

The reply was almost a whisper. "It wouldn't die. . . . I kept on . . . I didn't know where to aim."

Another silence.

"Did it die in the end?"

A pause. "Yes."

"What about the others?"

"I left them. I couldn't do it again. They'll just have to take their chance."

Jim was gripping the corner of a piece of sacking and wrenching at it.

"I'm sorry." Tony hesitated awkwardly. "I must get back to Number One. It's nearly his turn to go over to the harbor. I'm sorry."

He turned and shambled, stiff-legged, away. His half-dry trousers were like cardboard.

Poor old beggars, he thought. *We don't know enough about them. Perhaps everything we've done so far is wrong. Perhaps they're all going to die and we'll have made it worse, carting them about instead of leaving them in peace. Perhaps they meant to strand. Perhaps they wish we'd leave them alone.*

Full of misgivings, he returned to Number One.

"How is he?"

"Just the same. Taking it easy."

As Tony took up his position beside the whale, the great head swung around sideways and butted his leg. He reached down and gripped the edge of the flipper.

"Hello," he said, and the blowhole snorted. *Well,* he thought, he *seems to be glad we're here anyway.*

Mom arrived soon afterward with a tote bag.

"I've got all sorts of clothes and a towel here, but for now you might as well just change into shorts."

"We'll form a circle around you so that nobody sees," said Tracey, grinning.

"Not likely," said Tony. He managed the whole operation with the aid of the towel wrapped discreetly round his waist, but it threatened to fall off halfway through.

"Can't think what you're fussing about," said Mom, "you've still got your underpants on."

"Yes, but everything's so wet, the whole lot tends to come off together."

"Well, quickly, then, there's a four-wheel drive on its way here, so I imagine it's time to shift this whale."

The truck swept around and back so that its wheels were in the water and its back pointed seaward, about eight yards directly inshore from Number One. Most of the ten or so men on the back stayed sprawled in an exhausted jumble of weary limbs, sodden clothing, and sand-stiffened hair. Jim and Graeme climbed from the cab and waded through the shallow water to where Tony now stood, back with Tracey, Carol, and the whale.

"Look, I'm not sure about this one," said Jim. "It doesn't look at all well to me, the way it's been just floating there for over four hours. I should have thought it would have gotten itself together and swum away by now. Everyone's worn out with all this lifting—it's not an easy job. I've been wondering whether just to give this one a push and encourage it to swim out to sea from here, but Graeme won't agree."

"It'd end up on the rocks, wouldn't it?" said Tony. "I know everyone's tired, but we three can help with this one. We've been stuck here doing nothing all this time, so we've got stacks of energy."

"Speak for yourself," said Tracey. "I'm worn out, and I'm supposed to be going out tonight," but she grinned and patted the whale, and Tony knew she would help.

There were sighs and grunts as the tired men on the truck eased themselves stiffly off into the water and pulled a large tarpaulin toward Number One. The tarpaulin was easily passed under the whale's body—his tail moved from side to side as he felt the cloth taking his weight, but otherwise he lay still. Tony, gripping part of the edge of the tarpaulin, bent and peered into the watchful eye.

"It's all right. You're going to be all right."

They swung the whale around so that its head was directed toward the truck. So far, so good, but this was the easy part, because the great body was still being supported by the water. When they tried to lift the tarpaulin with its load, seawater was trapped in with the whale, converting the expanse of canvas into a great sagging bag, far too heavy for them to manage.

"Lower it at the back," called Jim. "Let it drain out."

Carol and Graeme, who held the end of the tarpaulin supporting the great tail, dipped their hands right down.

"Now, Ted and Chris, let your bit down a little. Not too much! Don't want it sliding off."

Tony, up near the front, clenched his teeth and took as much of the weight as he could.

"Easy, son," said the man next to him, "we haven't started yet."

"Right," said Jim, "that's most of the water gone, I think. Up and forward. Ready . . . now!"

Up went the whale in a sudden surge as straining forearms raised him to the height of the truck. There was a staggering, shambling lurch sideways, and Tony lost his hold of the tarpaulin in his effort not to trip over the legs of the man beside him. The whale had been swung forward in its sling and its head rested on the truck. Tony realized with shame that he hadn't really taken any of the weight at all—he wasn't as tall as the others, and his arms weren't the right length.

"Oh, no!" gasped Carol, clutching part of the tail. She had lost the tarpaulin and was trembling under the weight of the fluke, knees bent. Tony started to run back to help her and nearly fell flat, the water dragging at his legs and almost tripping him. He rescued the tarpaulin, and together they took the strain. He could understand her sudden alarm; from this end, the whale appeared to be sloping

45

downhill and about to slip off the truck at any minute, to hit the surface of the water with a great bellyflop.

"It's okay," he said, panting. "I don't think he's going to slide off."

Four men were now stationed on the back of the truck, ready to pull the whale on.

"Ready . . ." called Jim. "Now!"

Those still in the water stumbled doggedly forward, bearing the whale with them. Now it was positioned as far forward on the truck as it would go. Leaving the blowhole clear, they covered the whale with wet sacking.

"Okay," said Graeme. "Tony, you walk behind and keep an eye on the tail. We'll be going very slowly. If you think the tail's going to bump into anything, give a shout and we'll stop immediately. Tracey and Carol, are you coming too?"

"Have you got enough helpers over at the harbor without me?" asked Tracey.

"Oh, yes, I think so, thanks, for the moment anyway."

"Well, then, I'll go home and wash my hair."

"I ought to get back to the milk bar," said Carol. "Mom's on her own up there, and it's supposed to be her day off."

"Okay. Sorry we can't give you a lift; we'll be loaded up enough as it is."

"Thanks for looking after him and everything," said Tony.

"No problem," said Tracey. "See you later."

Graeme organized four of the men to travel alongside the whale on the back of the truck, then started the engine. Mom appeared beside Tony, rummaging in her tote bag and producing a parka.

"Here, wear this. It's nearly evening and you'll get pneumonia."

Tony was quite glad to put it on, and even more pleased to find a piece of cheese and a jam tart thrust into his hand.

"Sorry it's such an odd mixture—I was in a hurry."

"Thanks, Mom."

Tony proudly took his place beside the tail, which was jutting out diagonally behind, and they set off over the sand. The cheese and jam tart tasted quite good together. Jim and the other men had turned and walked back toward the Land Rover and the huddled shapes of the two dead whales. They would be leaving someone in charge of the two corpses, to keep dogs and children away, and the rest of them would make their way over to the harbor.

As this, the last live whale, left the beach, there was a murmured cheer from all those who had worked or watched for so long. Many of the helpers who had been sluicing the other whales had already started to drift away—some to go home, most to go to the harbor—but enough still remained to hand their buckets up to the men who sat beside Number One on the truck. Others ran alongside, giving him a last douse of water as he started on his overland journey.

CHAPTER

5

~~~~~~~~~~~

THERE WAS A RHYTHMIC BUMPING as the wheels started over the transverse wooden slats that marked the beginning of the rise to the track. The noise of the engine changed pitch as Graeme eased the vehicle up the slope. They passed through a belt of ti trees, and Tony had to run ahead and hold a branch back so that it wouldn't injure the whale's tail. Out on the open road he felt elated walking beside a motorized whale. Some motorists had already stopped to watch and called out encouragement; but others, new on the scene, didn't know what was happening.

"Is it real?"

"Is it alive?"

"What are you trying to do?"

"That's not allowed, surely?"

Fortunately, he had to keep moving, so he merely smiled, muttered something noncommittal in answer to their questions, and left the motorists to explain it to each other as best they could.

The town was quite close at hand.

One of the men on the truck passed a bucket down to Tony so that he could pour water over Number One's tail. The others dampened the sacking over the body. They would be able to replenish the buckets in the town.

They began to pass houses. A row of spectators was sitting on a low wall—David's grandparents, looking after his three little sisters. They all cheered and waved. Tony grinned bashfully.

All they need is a few flags and some colored streamers, he thought.

Mrs. Hands leaned out of her bedroom window and watched them go past.

"Is that the last one?"

"Yes."

Tony had been born in this town and had never lived in any other house but the one over by the bay. He knew these streets, these hedges, these walls. He knew individual plants—the clump of knotgrass and capeweed around the lamppost, the fronds of the peppertree on the corner. They were part of him. Now, walking along the road beside the tail of a whale, he could observe the people who watched. He could see them and their town as an outsider would. It was a good place. A community.

They all care about the whales, he thought. *We're all together in this.*

They passed along the deserted main street and stopped at the garage for water to dampen the sacking. There was the sound of a horn as Jim's Land Rover drove past on its way to the harbor.

Daylight was beginning to fade as they turned down toward the harbor. Tony shivered. Still damp, and in places downright soaking, his clothes clung to him unpleasantly. His sneakers had squirted out most of their surplus water and were now just heavy and cloying. Without the parka, he would have frozen.

Down by the harbor, most of the inhabitants of the town were standing or sitting along the wall, on the quay and on the hill behind. The long, lean shapes of the whales in the calm water looked markedly unfishlike seen from above; their horizontal tails projected sideways unlike any fish's. They lay suspended in the shallow part of the harbor, each attended by two or three men nearly up to their waists in the water. Farther out, two rowboats were stationed between the whales and the open sea.

Graeme reversed the truck slowly down a concrete

ramp to the harbor's edge and drove no farther. The muddy, clinging sand, unpleasant for legs, was treacherous for wheels. Tony's sneakers disappeared, bubbling and wheezing. He wrenched them free again and slopped up the concrete slope until he was level with Number One's head.

"Hello," said Tony. There was no response, no movement of the eye confronting him.

"Okay," said Graeme. "Last one."

Helpers gathered around and grasped the tarpaulin.

"Tony, you'd better stand back for this, thanks all the same. You're just not tall enough, and it's tricky getting them off without zonking them under the chin with the back of the truck—we did that to one of them and it squealed! There are far more people to help now than we had on the beach."

"Don't worry, Tony," said his dad, "I'll hold him up single-handed if the others drop him."

Tony, standing on the ramp, was joined by Sam.

"That's your whale, isn't it? The one you've been with all the time."

"Yes, he's the last. Anything special been happening over here?"

"Not really. They've all been unloaded okay, though one of the early ones landed with a bit of a bump—it was so blooming big and heavy. See that Rolls over there? Some guy was driving past, saw one of the whales coming overland, and he's been here ever since, taking photos and helping with the . . ."

Graeme's call of "Ready!" broke into the chatter.

"Now!"

The whale was shifted back until quite a large proportion of its body was supported only by the tarpaulin. Tony counted nine, eleven, thirteen men along one side, there must have been about twenty-six of them altogether, all tense and preparing for the next concerted effort.

"Ready . . . now!"

Number One was moved backward, free of the truck,

and was lowered—rather too quickly, Tony felt—to the ground. The men didn't straighten up but, still gripping the tarpaulin, shifted the whale back in a series of short bursts of effort until it lay in the water, with its belly only just clear of the mud. Then at last they straightened up and relaxed, and several of them walked away.

"They'll leave him like that for a while," explained Sam, "just to get used to the water, and to get over the shock of the journey."

"Let's go down and have a look at him."

"No, I'll wait here. I reckon when you've seen one whale, you've seen them all."

Tony sloshed through the mud. He wished he could bring Number One something to eat. All the whales must be very hungry by now. They mustn't be kept here too long or their hunger might make them too weak to swim.

Ten or eleven men had stayed with Number One and were gently rocking him from side to side and rubbing and stroking him.

"Why are you rocking him?"

"Apparently it helps them to get their balance back and to get used to being in the water. Some fellow has arrived from the Friends of the Whales group. He's seen strandings before; he seems to know what to do, and he said we should rock them."

"He wasn't on the beach, was he?"

"No, he turned up in the town, and they sent him straight down here to the harbor. That's him over there, talking to Jim Russell and Howard. The one with the red jacket."

"What happens next?"

"That's probably what they're trying to decide now. The idea is to keep all the whales here for the night anyway, now that it's getting dark, and get them all moving first thing tomorrow when we can see what we're doing and the tide's right. It will also give the whales a chance to get their strength back during the cool of the night."

"But they're not going to be left alone during the night?"

"No, we'll have to take it in turns to stand with them. It's going to be hellish cold."

"Well, I'll stay with this one; he's the one I've been with all along."

"I think you'll find they're only going to ask people who have wetsuits. You couldn't possibly stand in the water during the night if you didn't have a wetsuit—not without getting double pneumonia, anyway."

After a while Howard called a meeting in the parking lot by the quayside. He introduced Jim Russell and the Friends of the Whales man, Terry something. Jim gave an account of the progress so far; two whales had been left dead on the beach, four were on the rocks, either dead or probably nearly so, and thirteen were here in the harbor. At first light they would be encouraged to leave.

"How?" asked somebody. "They don't seem to want to go. They're all pretty lethargic."

"We'll just have to play it by ear. Maybe we can drive them out like sheep—or we may have to tow them out. Meanwhile, we must draw up a roster for watching duty through the night. Each whale needs someone standing alongside, and we need a few extras on call in case of emergency. We've decided people shouldn't be in the water during the night if they haven't got wetsuits, but we already know of some people who have volunteered to let someone else have a turn with their wetsuit while they themselves get some sleep."

Josh was delegated to collect names and organize some kind of schedule for the night.

"I suppose there's nobody with a wetsuit my size?" Tony asked him.

"Doesn't look like it, I'm afraid."

"Well, I'll wait on the quay and watch from there."

"And get unnecessarily cold, tired, and bored, most likely. With a bit of luck there'll be nothing to see; the whales will just mooch about, the way they're doing now."

"But I can't go home. It would take me half an hour to get back here if anything happened, even running all the way."

"I tell you what, sleep at our house for the night. Sue'll find you a sleeping bag, and your dad can get a message to you quickly if anything happens. I've got his name down to take turns using my wetsuit, and I'll put us down to look after your whale—it's that one with the chunk out of its tail, isn't it?"

Tony accepted reluctantly but gratefully. The street-lights came on, and lights were switched on in the houses on the quayside, to improve visibility as much as possible. Some of the small boats bobbing on the water had lighted cabins or had lamps at their mastheads, and a searchlight on a trawler momentarily seared a path across the water where the whales lay. It wouldn't be used continuously all night, but was in position ready for immediate use if required.

Tony and his parents sat on the harbor wall and ate fish and chips. None of them had had any money on them, but the proprietor of the fish shop was allowing credit just this once, and trade was booming. Tony wrapped his legs more tightly in a towel from Mom's capacious tote bag, but couldn't disguise a shiver.

"That last big group of whales that all came in together," said Mom, "they were all milling around in circles on the surface of the water offshore for ages before they all decided to head for the beach. Mrs. Hawsworth and I could see them."

"Waiting for the ones on the beach to come back, most likely," said Dad. "Terry says the ones already stranded send out distress calls, and the others in the water won't leave them. Then they start coming in in groups to try to help them."

"Aren't the ones on the rocks going to call back this lot when they leave the harbor tomorrow morning?" asked Tony.

"The vet's going to make sure all four are dead before then."

"Not shoot them?"

"No, apparently he was going to give them an injection, but Terry says they'll soon die naturally anyway."

The sky changed from green to inky blue. They sat for a while longer, then Mom sighed and gathered up all the empty fish-and-chip wrappers.

"I'm going home now, but I'll be back first thing in the morning. Get some sleep, Tony, there's nothing happening."

Tony went for a last look at Number One. The whale's belly was clear of the mud, and he hung lazily in the water beside Josh. Mom was right; nothing was happening.

Sue and the baby were in the kitchen when Tony knocked at the back door. The bright light and the warmth were overpowering. Suddenly he desperately needed to sleep. He could barely keep awake in the shower as he rinsed off the sticky encrustation of salt and sand. The sleeping bag was luxuriously dry and smooth. He cocooned himself in the warmth of it and was asleep.

CHAPTER

6

‸‸‸‸‸‸‸‸‸‸‸‸

DESPITE THE DEPTH OF HIS SLEEP, Tony woke abruptly while it was still dark, thinking, "Whales!" He wriggled out of the sleeping bag, nearly losing Josh's pajama trousers in the process, and peered at the clock on the mantelpiece. Ten past five; time to get going. He crept through to the hall and saw a light under the kitchen door. Sue was sitting at the kitchen table, nursing the baby and reading a book.

"Have you been here all the time?" he asked.

"No, but we've had a bad night. I think she's teething. Didn't you hear all the crying? I was afraid it would wake you. Look, here are some of David's clothes; I borrowed them from his mother after you'd gone to bed. She says they'll fit you all right. Yours are in a terrible state."

"Oh, thanks, that's great, but I might as well wear my own shoes and socks, since they'll get wet right away in any case. Do you know what's happening with the whales?"

"Nothing much, as far as I know. Josh came in for a while to get warm, and your father was here about half an hour ago. Apparently it's just a question of standing about, waiting for daylight. They said to tell you that your whale's fine. There was a bit of trouble with one of the others, though—she kept sinking and had to be held up. Terry told them to keep rocking her and moving her tail up and down, and she seems to have recovered now."

The sky was beginning to lighten at the horizon, but the main source of illumination was still the street lamps and the glow from windows. The thirteen whales lay in the water of the harbor. The tide was fairly high, and the whales were close inshore, each attended by at least one person.

"What happens next?" Tony called down to Howard, who was standing waist deep alongside the largest whale, patting and rubbing it and talking to it in a soothing, low voice.

"We try to encourage them to go. We're just getting a few boats organized, then we're going to get started."

Tony waded in to join his father beside Number One. David's clothes didn't stay dry for long, he thought.

"Idiot," called Dad. "Don't come any farther. There's nothing for you to do here anyway."

"I've got to come and say good-bye to him."

"You're crazy, you know that?"

As before, the whale swung slightly around and gently nudged Tony.

"You see? How could I *not* come?" Suddenly he wanted to throw his arms around the whale and ride out to sea on its back.

The creak and clunk of oars in rowlocks caught his attention, and he looked up to see Josh positioning his dinghy at the side of the harbor. Soon there were two more dinghies and four kayaks. They were maneuvered into a line between the whales and the land.

"Right," called Jim. "Try to get the whales moving seaward."

Dad stood behind Number One's flipper and walked slowly forward through the water, pushing gently against the flipper.

"Good-bye. Oh, good-bye," said Tony, with a terrible, desperate longing. He walked on the other side of the whale until he was out of his depth, then he swam, gently propelling himself with his legs, while his hand rested on the whale's back.

"We must leave him now," said Dad. "They're going to have to start herding them out, and we could get hurt if the whales start bunching together."

"Safe journey," whispered Tony, and stroked the great back for the last time. He turned reluctantly and swam with his father back to the cordon of little boats. The whales were unattended, idling gently in a haphazard group. Occasionally a blowhole would emit a quiet snort, rather like a contented horse.

At a call from Jim there was sudden noise and activity among the boats. The dinghies and kayaks were turned and eased out toward the whales. In the water between them several men lay on surfboards paddling themselves onward through the water with their hands. The chain of boats, boards, and people closed in on the whales, with much splashing and shouting.

"Go on!"

"Move, will you?"

The men on the surfboards smacked the surface of the water with the flat of their hands. Oars and paddles rose dripping and flashing in the dawn light before descending onto the water with a resounding thwack and sheet of spray.

The whales continued to float aimlessly, giving no more than the slightest movement of a flipper or of their powerful tails. One by one they began to drift back through gaps in the cordon of boats.

"No good," said Jim. "We'll have to try towing."

"What, all of them?"

"No, with a bit of luck we shall only need to tow one of them out and the others'll follow. Let's use the one that was the first to strand."

"Which one was that?" asked Terry, the man from the Friends of the Whales.

"Look, I'm not sure where he is just at this minute, but we can soon find out; he's a young one with a chunk out of his tail."

"Is he in fairly good condition?"

"Well, to tell you the truth, he didn't look too good yesterday. He was out of the water the longest and seemed to take quite a time to recover. Shock and exposure or something, I suppose. Seems okay now, though."

"Even so, sounds as though he might be a bad choice for the tow. Whichever one we choose has got to have the strength to get its blowhole above the surface even when it's traveling backward through the water. This one you're talking about might have lost the will to try. Might be a better bet to tow the big one. I gather it was the first of that last batch of fourteen to strand, and, as it happens, it was the first back through our cordon just now; the others were happy enough just milling about until it shot through, then they gradually all meandered back after it, including the notch-tailed one. Could be they'll follow it again, only this time out to sea."

Sacking was wound around the narrow part of the body of the biggest whale, the tail stock. A rope was carefully tied around this and attached to the stern of Graeme's fishing boat; Terry was worried about the possibility of the rope chafing the whale's flesh and hoped that the sacking would provide some protection. All the dinghies, kayaks, and surfboards were moved out of the way, and Graeme very slowly edged the vessel toward the mouth of the harbor. As he took up the slack of the rope and the whale started to be drawn backward through the water, Terry swam beside it, watching carefully for any sign of distress or difficulty. As they progressed gradually farther and farther away, all the little boats assembled again behind the rest, ready to shepherd them out. Slowly the mass of dark shapes began to slide gracefully seaward after their leader.

"It's working!"

"The big one's calling them out!"

"There they go!"

There was a sudden yell from farther out in the harbor. Terry was frantically waving his arms above his head and yelling at Graeme. The boat lost what little speed it had had and idled, bobbing and tipping gently on the slight swell while Graeme and Terry communicated with each other in a series of shouts and gesticulations. The movement of the group of whales had become aimless again.

"What are they doing? Why don't they get going again? We're going to have all the whales back inshore again if they don't get a move on."

Josh rowed his dinghy out to Graeme's boat, giving the free-swimming whales a wide berth. Tony, soaked to the skin as usual, ran along to the end of the harbor wall to see if he could make out what was happening. There had been no colorful sunrise, but the sky had lightened to a uniform silvery gray; Terry could be seen climbing onto the fishing vessel, and the three men seemed to be having a conference about something. They were taking an infuriatingly long time. The rope was stretched down over the stern and passed down into the dark water; there was no sign of the big whale tied to the other end. She had evidently stopped sending signals to the others. There was no longer any unifying purpose behind their indolent movements.

The engine of Graeme's boat gained in power, and the hull swung slowly around in a graceful arc as he steered it toward its mooring place at the side of the harbor. The rope at the stern was still taut as it towed the heavy whale back again. Under the surface! What was the whale doing? It should be visible now and then breaking the surface of the water as it came up to breathe. Tony ran back along the wall and was waiting at the steps when Graeme eased the boat into position beside them.

"What's happening? Why have you come back?"

"Whale's drowned."

"No! Surely not! Can't we do something?"

"No, it's had it. Terry even tried to hold it up in the water, but there was never a chance. It didn't seem to have the willpower to try to help itself."

Terry was hunched over the rail at the bow, staring moodily at the water.

"It's tough on him," said Graeme quietly. "He seems to care about them a lot."

"Well, we all do, don't we?"

"Yes, of course. Look, help me tie this one up, can you? We'll need to leave her ready for the vet to have a look at. There's some idea that whales might strand because parasitic worms have made them ill, though Terry says that's more likely to be the case when just one strands, not when there's a whole group like this. Anyway, the vet'll want to take samples from this one and from the others over on the beach and the rocks."

The rope attached to the whale's tail was tied to a mooring chain and the great corpse floated just below the surface of the water. It moved slightly with the movement of the water. As Tony stared at it, the body seemed to have life in it.

"Are you sure it's dead?"

"Quite sure. Come aboard if you like."

"Thanks."

Tony looked out across the harbor. The rest of the whales were quite active now, cutting through the water with majestic ease.

They don't belong in such an enclosed space, he thought. *They're cramped, like racing swimmers in a garden pool. If we could just get them out into the sea, there'd be no stopping them; they're ready to go.*

They showed no interest in the harbor entrance, though. In fact one or two of them had already returned to the shallower water near the dinghies and kayaks.

"What can we do?"

It was Terry who answered. "We're going to see if we can use the trawler to take two of them out frontward, slung in tarpaulins from the booms. That way their motion through the water should be more natural to them, and there's less likelihood that they'll drown. Josh has gone to organize it now. I gather the owner's somewhere around, and at least three of the crew are over there on the quayside. It may be a bit of a problem catching the two whales, though. Let's hope they've quietened down a bit by the time we're ready. Then we aim to use the two whales the same way we were trying to use the big one—they'll send out signals that the rest will follow, and that way we'll get them all out to the open sea. We might as well make sure one of the two we take is that notch-tailed one who stranded first; they might be more likely to follow him."

"Oh, no, please, not Number One; he'll drown."

"Not going out frontward, he won't. Don't worry, he'll be all right. We took the big one out too fast; we ought to have stopped every now and then, to let her breathe. I wish I'd thought of the trawler before. We know so little about whale strandings, you see. It's all very much trial and error, and I've never been involved before in getting whales out of a harbor; it's a bit different from getting them away from a beach. I must go and help organize the two whales for the trawler now. Graeme, can you stand by ready to help herd the others out?"

"Sure. What about you, Tony. Do you want to stay here or will you go on the trawler?"

"I'll go and see Number One. Then, when the trawler goes out, I'll swim along beside him; I can hang on to the tarpaulin."

"No, sorry, that's out of the question," said Terry. "A drowned whale's bad enough, we don't want any drowned people. This whale-rescue thing mustn't get out of proportion. We'll do what we can for them, but not at the expense of human lives."

"But you swam with the big one."

"First of all, I'm a strong swimmer wearing a wetsuit. Second, I've had more experience, and there was the chance I might have been able to help—I only wish I could have. Third, I'm responsible for myself, whereas if anything happened to you, your father would lynch me. And fourth, I'm inconsistent."

"Tell you what," said Graeme. "Go and see Number One, and when the trawler's ready to go, come back here and help me with the boat. I've got binoculars—you can keep an eye on Number One."

"Okay, thanks," said Tony ruefully.

He and Terry jumped ashore and walked around to the town end of the harbor, where the whales were again congregating.

"What's so special about this notch-tailed one?"

"Oh, well, I found him first thing yesterday morning on the beach, when he was the only one. I kind of got to know him, I suppose. Sometimes it even seems as though he recognizes me—he nudges my legs when I get back to him after I've been away. Is that possible, do you think?"

"Oh, definitely. They're very intelligent, you know. There's no reason why they shouldn't recognize us just as we recognize them."

"But sometimes I've been in trousers and sometimes in shorts."

"Doesn't matter. There's your size, and the way you move—and maybe he finds those sneakers unforgettable—I certainly would!"

Tony looked down at the bloated gray fungal masses encasing his feet. The lace holes bubbled and spluttered as he walked.

For a few hours last night I was dry, he thought. *What luxury.*

There were plenty of people ringing the harbor now; those who had gone home to bed had returned. Although it was Monday morning, there wouldn't be much work done while the whales were still there.

Dad was already standing by Number One. Tony put his hand on the whale's back and said hello. The blowhole snorted loudly. Tony told Dad about the decision that Number One was to be one of the two whales to be taken out by the trawler—"But I wish they wouldn't."

"I don't know. I can't see that he'd come to any harm, going out frontward."

63

"But if we help to hitch him to the trawler and then he drowns, we will have killed him, won't we?"

"Don't exaggerate. We will have done our best; we can't do any more. Here they come now."

The trawler's engine had started up, although it was another minute before the hull edged slowly away from the quay and drew out in front of the group of whales. A tarpaulin sling hung from each boom. When the trawler was in position, the booms dropped and the two slings slopped quietly into the water and floated slackly. Men on surfboards paddled over with their hands and held one of

the slings open and ready. Kayaks and dinghies lined up to
form a route from Number One to the sling.

"Okay," called Howard from the deck of the trawler,
"see if he'll go."

"That's us," said Dad. "Come on!"

They moved forward and were very soon out of their
depth, swimming beside the whale. People behind them
slapped the water and shouted to encourage the whale
onward. He slipped silently into the area of water enclosed
by the sling and stopped, his way barred by two crossed
paddles. The men waiting for him lashed the tarpaulin

loosely around his body, in front of and behind the dorsal fin and behind the flippers.

"Fine," called Howard. "Now the other one."

The surfboards were assembled around the other sling, and the small boats again formed an avenue, this time to the nearest whale, since it didn't matter which whale was used now that Number One was safely in his harness.

Tony swam to land, raced back along the harbor wall, and leaped onto Graeme's boat.

"Careful, you'll break your neck—those shoes look slippery. Here are the binoculars. Terry's coming any minute. He's decided to come with us because we've got speed and maneuverability. Here he is."

They veered away from the mooring; the body of the drowned whale, tied to the mooring chain, swayed in their bow wave as if heaving a great sigh. A hundred yards away, the trawler headed slowly for the open sea, gently towing its precious double load from its raised booms like a milkmaid with pails on a yoke. Two men swam with each whale to keep it steady. Tony focused the binoculars on the sling in which Number One was cradled, but he couldn't honestly see very much. Although the deck on which he stood felt steady enough when he looked around him with the naked eye, as soon as he tried to peer through the binoculars, his field of vision tossed and lurched alarmingly. Graeme didn't follow the trawler but steered them back behind the remaining whales, which were being gently edged forward by the small boats and surfboards.

"They're not going, are they?" said Tony. "It's not working. Perhaps the two with the trawler have drowned already."

He was aware that his voice sounded brightly matter-of-fact.

"Let's go and have a look," said Terry.

When they reached the trawler, at the mouth of the harbor, they could see that both whales were still alive. Terry called over, asking for the engine to be stopped. "Perhaps the noise of the engine's putting them off."

Graeme switched off his engine too, and the two boats drifted in the sudden silence. As Tony's ears grew accustomed to the lack of the pounding throb of the boats, they distinguished squeaking calls from Number One and the other whale.

"The others must surely hear. Why don't they come?"

"Turn them around," said Terry. Then "Turn them around!" he shouted to Howard on the deck of the trawler, as he let himself down over the side of Graeme's boat. "Stay there," he said to Tony, who looked ready to follow. Terry guided and steadied each tarpaulin in turn until each whale was now facing back toward the others in the harbor. There was a distant shout from the crowd of people on the shore two hundred yards away, and the little boats started to move nearer.

"They're coming," roared Howard.

Soon black shapes appeared and disappeared in the water as the undulating backs broke the surface and submerged again.

"Look at them go," sighed Tony. "They're beautiful."

The two whales in the trawler slings were released by the men who had swum beside them; they wheeled in a banking turn and joined the rest of the group, cleaving their way to the open sea. Number One swam with strength and grace—a healthy young whale fully recovered after his ordeal in a strange environment.

Tony watched until they were out of sight and remained straining against the rail of the boat staring out to sea. Occasionally a dark shape appeared fleetingly on the shimmering silver expanse, and he thought he saw a whale's dorsal fin and sleek back curve up and over at the peak of its sinuous swimming lope, but the sea was slightly choppy, and black shadows came and went with the play of light on the wavelets. In truth, the whales were probably already lost to view.

Graeme started the engine. Terry climbed aboard and they headed back to the mooring. Tony felt desperately lonely; he longed to believe that he might see Number One again, but at the same time he knew that if he did, it would mean that the whale had stranded again.

No, he thought, *I mustn't want to see him again. I must concentrate hard on the thought that he's gone to live a natural whale's life, free in the ocean. He doesn't need human beings anymore.*

People started to drift away into the town. Now that the need for activity and effort had passed, many were feeling wet, cold, and tired. There was a general yearning for a relaxing shower, a hot meal, and bed, but many of them would have to shower quickly, pull on some dry clothes, and go to work. Tiredness was mingled with a sense of satisfaction, of achievement.

Katie's mother gave Tony and his parents a lift home. Tony and his father had to sit on newspapers so that they wouldn't make the car sears wet and salty.

"No school today, I think," said Dad. "I'm sure they'll understand."

"Thanks. I'll go down to the beach, then, to see if the vet's done anything about the whales there and on the rocks."

"He's there now. Jim's gone to join him. But I don't think they'll want any spectators. I think they'd appreciate it far more if they were left alone. They've got to do a bit of dissecting to take samples, and I'm sure they don't want a crowd of people breathing down their necks."

"I'm not a crowd."

"Tony, let them get on with their work on their own."

"Okay. Have we got any books about whales?"

"There'd be a bit in the encyclopedia. Then it'd be a case of trying at the library."

"I wonder why they do it."

"Strand? I don't know. Jim was saying there's some new theory that they might be confused by local variations in magnetic fields—something to do with iron in the rocks upsetting their navigation system. Nobody knows."

Although it was midmorning when they reached home, bed was very inviting.

"Something to eat first," suggested Mom. "An omelet would be quick."

Tony slept right through from midday until the early hours of the following morning.

CHAPTER

7

TONY LAY WAITING FOR IT TO GET LIGHT, thinking about the whales and running through in his mind all that had happened. He wondered where Number One was now. Weaving effortlessly through the water, back in his element. He thought back to his first sight of the whale, just after . . . just after he had found the paper nautilus. He sat up in bed. The shells were still on the dunes.

He dressed quickly and let himself out the back door. Once he was outside, the sky seemed lighter than it had appeared when seen from his bedroom window. Quite light enough to find the starkly white nautilus, anyway. As he set off over the grass, he suddenly had a deep dread that history would repeat itself and that Number One would again be stranded on the beach—this time, dead.

Oh, let him not be there. I couldn't bear it if he were there dead.

From the top of the slope leading to the beach, he could scan the flat crescent of sand. Nothing. No whales, not even the two dead ones—what had they done with those? The relief was immense. He ran down the slope and along the beach toward the place where he had found Number One. But where had that been, exactly? He looked up at the dunes at the back, trying to pick out the one on which he had left the shells. As he walked along and changed the angle from which he looked at each dune, it changed its shape. The crests were tufted and leaning like camels' humps. Which was the one? Where had Mom and

Mrs. Hawsworth been standing? He tried to visualize them standing against the sky, waving their arms and pointing at the whales that were being swept onto the rocks. But he hadn't noticed the shape of the dunes. He tried to remember where he had run to pee, but he had been too preoccupied at the time to notice the landscape. He'd just have to get up on the dunes and search the tops, one by one.

The marram grass rustled and rattled in the gray breeze, and runnels of sand hissed down the dune slopes. He toiled up each crest and scoured the clumps of marram for the cache of shells. There was no sign of them. He must have passed the place by now. Turning, he worked his way back along the ridge. How could they all have disappeared? Could the wind have blown the sand so much that they had been completely covered? Was he searching in the wrong place? Had somebody found the shells and taken them? Surely not—they would have known the shells belonged to someone, wouldn't they? Perhaps someone had found them, guessed that they were wanted, and had taken them to a safe place? Unlikely.

There was a shout from the beach below. Howard and Ruff were jogging along the high-water mark. Tony leaped down the dune to meet them.

"What's happened to the two dead whales?"

"They've been carted away. The museum wants parts of their skeletons, not to go on show but for study."

"Did the vet find any parasitic worms?"

"Only one or two—not enough to explain the stranding."

"Well, I wonder why they stranded then."

"I dunno. Terry said some chap in New Zealand thinks maybe sometimes there's some kind of an upset among a group of whales—a sort of family row, I suppose, and one of them goes off in a huff and gets himself stuck."

"That'd have been Number One?"

"Yeah, that's right. If so, the argument seems to be over—they all swam off quite amicably together, didn't they."

"Any sign of them since?"

"No, thank goodness. Looks as though they're well away. Is that what you were doing up on the dunes—looking for whales?"

"Well, partly, yes, but looking for my shells as well— you remember I had a bag of them. There was a nautilus. I've been trying to find one for years, and now I don't know what's happened to it."

"Looking in the wrong place, most likely."

"No. I've been all along the stretch where they could possibly be."

"Someone's taken them, then."

"That's what I thought, but surely not. I mean, everybody was working together so well on the beach. Even the kids who don't normally join in things were helping. We all belonged together, d'you know what I mean? Surely none of them would have stolen my shells? They'd have asked around, to see if anybody claimed them."

"I dunno, some people are always going to put themselves first, however much community spirit there is. Look, down in the city there are plenty of shell shops; I'll look out for a nautilus for you next time I'm there."

"Thanks, that's very kind, but it wouldn't be the same. Buying one, I mean. This one was special because I found it—you know? That made it extra-specially mine."

"Yeah, I know what you mean. But, look, you found something better than that, you found a whale. Forget about that old shell—it's only a cast-off old egg case anyway. Think of your whale out there in the Pacific somewhere. He's a young one, so he might live nearly as long as you do. They say whales are very intelligent; I'll bet he'll remember you, just as you'll remember him, for as long as you both live. Isn't that a lot more special than some old shell?"

Tony turned and looked out over the sea.

"Yes, it is," he said. And smiled.